MacGooses' Grocery

by Frank Asch · pictures by James Marshall

THE DIAL PRESS · NEW YORK

The Dial Press
1 Dag Hammarskjold Plaza
New York, New York 10017

Text copyright © 1978 by Frank Asch
Pictures copyright © 1978 by James Marshall
All rights reserved | First Printing
Printed in the United States of America
Typography by Atha Tehon

Library of Congress Cataloging in Publication Data
Asch, Frank.
MacGooses' Grocery.
Summary: Mother, Father, Junior, and Sis Goose get tired of
looking after the new egg, so the egg must look after itself.
[1. Geese–Fiction. 2. Eggs–Fiction]
I. Marshall, James, 1942– II. Title.
PZ7.A778Mac [E] 77-86270
ISBN 0-8037-5237-7 ISBN 0-8037-5231-8 lib. bdg.

To Robert Kraus
F.A.

For William James Gray
J.M.

The MacGooses owned a
grocery store and every day
they sat in it together
waiting for customers.

Mrs. MacGoose not only had to sit in the store, she had to sit on her new egg.

One day, Mrs. MacGoose got tired of sitting on her egg, so she put Mr. MacGoose in charge and went for a walk.

Soon Mr. MacGoose got tired of sitting on the egg,

so he put Junior in charge
and he went for a walk.

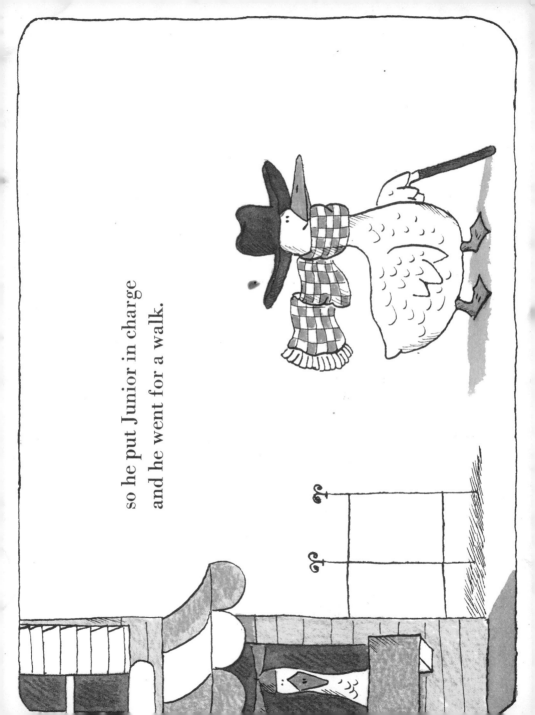

Soon Junior got tired,

so he put Sis in charge and he went for a walk.

Soon Sis got tired.

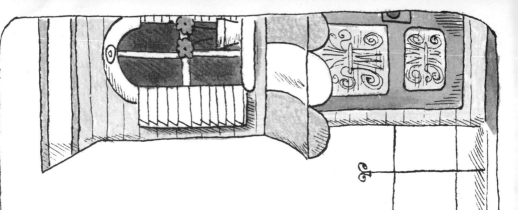

She put the egg in charge
and went for a walk.

With everyone gone, the baby inside the egg soon got cold.

He put on some warm clothes, but he was still cold.

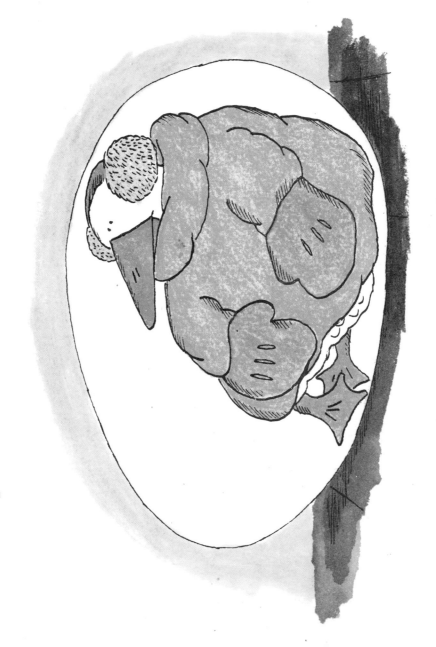

Just then some playful weasels
came into the store,
and seeing no one around,
they decided to have some fun.

They built mountains with all the food

. . . and knocked them down.

When the weasels heard the MacGooses coming, they ran out the back door, leaving the egg near the stove.

Soon it was so hot inside the egg that the baby goose had to take off all his clothes.

When Mrs. MacGoose got back and saw the mess, she nearly fainted.

"It's not my fault," said Father MacGoose, "I put Junior in charge."

"It's not my fault," said Junior, "I put Sis in charge."

"It's not my fault," said Sis, "I put the egg in charge."

Just then . . . .

. . . the egg hatched.

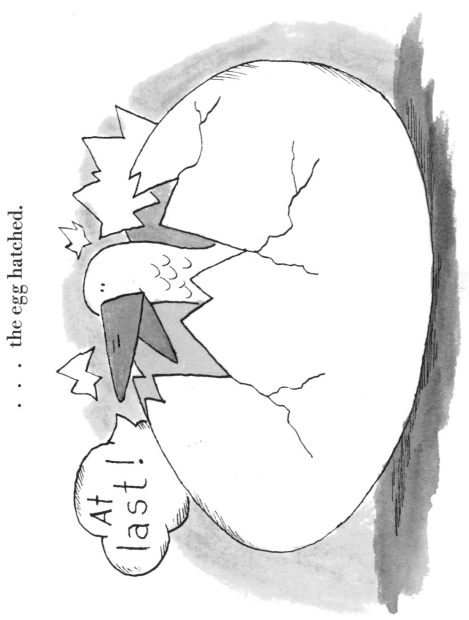

"Never mind whose fault it was," said Mother MacGoose. "It's too nice a day to worry about that sort of thing."

"That's right," said Father.

And they all went for a walk.